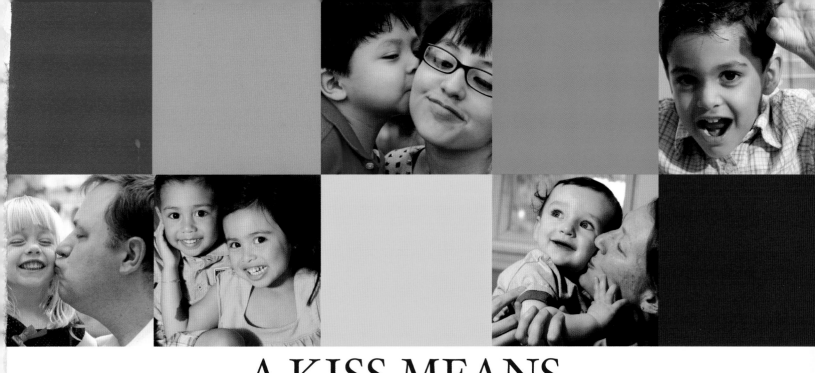

# A KISS MEANS
# I LOVE YOU

To my parents, Glenn and Ellen, with love.—K.M.A.

To Laura and all our kids.—E.F.

And to the beautiful children and their loved ones photographed
for this book . . . thank you.—K.M.A. and E.F.

Library of Congress Cataloging-in-Publication Data
Allen, Kathryn Madeline.
A kiss means I love you / by Kathryn Madeline Allen ; photographs by Eric Futran.
p. cm.
Summary: Explores the meanings of different actions, expressions, words,
and sounds, from a kiss and a clap to a wave and a yawn.
ISBN 978-0-8075-4186-9 (hardcover)
[1. Stories in rhyme. 2. Communication–Fiction.] I. Futran, Eric, ill. II. Title.
PZ8.3.A4188Kis 2012
[E]–dc23
2011034185

10  9  8  7  6  5  4  BP  17  16  15  14  13

The design is by Nick Tiemersma.

For more information about Albert Whitman & Company,
please visit our web site at www.albertwhitman.com.

# A KISS MEANS
# I LOVE YOU

Kathryn Madeline Allen     photographs by Eric Futran

ALBERT WHITMAN & COMPANY

CHICAGO, ILLINOIS

A kiss means
I love you,

a wave means hello,

a smile means I'm happy,

a tug means let's go!

A laugh
means it's
funny,

a cry means
I'm sad,

a *yum!* means I like it,

a pout means I'm mad.

A cheer means I did it!
Hurray!
I am proud!

A *shush* means
be quiet . . .

that's a
little too
loud!

A shiver means I'm chilly
(please warm me up quick).

A sniffle,
a sneeze,
and a cough
mean I'm sick.

A *roar!*
means
I'm scary,

a reach means
let's share,

a clap means I like it,

a hug means I care.

A yawn means
I'm sleepy

(please
tuck me
in tight).

A kiss means
I love you.

I love you . . . good night.